This book is dedicated to my beautiful Grandma. My Grandma loves cats and books as much as I do. She is my inspiration and I have her to thank so much. I am lucky to have shared so many memories with my best friend, my Grandma.

Grandma, love you lots!

To Zoe

I hope you enjoy my story about my cheeky cats and their adventures.
Remember, if you can dream it then you can achieve it.

Keep smiling.

Rebecca Jayne

2020

Jasper and Arlo are **best buddies.**

Jasper has black fur and amber-orange eyes.

His tail is **long** and **swishes** around.

Arlo has ginger fur, a stripy tail

and **sparkling** blue eyes.

He loves to **sneak** around.

Jasper and Arlo are **best friends.**

They have lots of **fun** and **love**

adventures.

The boys spend all of their time together.

They even have a secret language to talk to each other.

Big cats need to chat.

Jasper and Arlo love to **explore.**

Every day they find the **tallest** tree and

look up as **high** as can be.

Jasper **stretches** high and Arlo

copies him.

They stretch as far as they can reach.

Every **big** cat needs to **Stretch**

well to start the day.

Jasper and Arlo love to look **fierce.**

They find their favourite claw sharpener and attack.

Jasper digs his claws into the rock and scratches until they are sharp.

Arlo scratches until his claws are sharper.

Big cats need sharp claws.

Jasper and Arlo love to sound **scary.**

They sit proudly looking into the wild ready to

show off their growls.

Arlo takes a deep breath...**ROAR!**

He makes Jasper jump.

Jasper takes a deeper breath...**ROARRR!**

The birds flap their wings and fly away to safety.

Jasper and Arlo are **hungry** cats.

They sneak up to their food, **wiggle** their tails and **pounce!**

They **gobble** up their prey quickly and **slurp** their drink.

Big cats need lots of energy to stay **STRONG**.

Jasper and Arlo like to keep clean.

Brushing their teeth is important to keep

them **shiny.** Jasper and Arlo show their

Smiles   and check that they **sparkle.**

Big cats have award-winning smiles.

A toothy growl means it is time to go.

Jasper and Arlo are **adventurers**. They love to climb the highest mountains. Choosing the highest peak, Arlo **races** Jasper to the top.

Thump,

thump,

thump.

Jasper wins.

Big cats need to catch their breath ready for their next challenge.

Jasper and Arlo love to **solve mysteries.**

They sneak up to the **rushing** waterfall and nod

to each other.

Today it is Arlo's turn to try and find where the water

comes from.

Drip,

   drip,

      drip...splash!

Arlo falls into the lagoon and the waterfall **splats** on his head.

Big cats can giggle too.

Jasper and Arlo are proud of their home.

The wolves who live nearby **growl** at the boys

whenever they see them.

With a **skip** and a **jump**, the big cats parade around the perimeter.

They **hiss** at the wolves then run to safety.

Big cats always win.

Jasper and Arlo are **FIGHTERS**. They sneak, prowl and team up to ATTACK!

Defeated creatures are all around them.

Big cats are **brave** and the boys are now ready to approach

the **ULTIMATE ENEMY.**

Ready, steady...attack!

The boys launch themselves high into the air.

Oh no! They are caught by the enemy.

They cannot escape! What should they do?

Jasper and Arlo **love** the enemy really.

Human cuddles are the best.

With a **purr** and a **snuggle**, the **big** cat adventure is left for

another day

....

Jasper and Arlo are my wonderful, mischievous and loving cats who inspire my stories. Jasper loves bed time snuggles and hiding in boxes of all sizes. Arlo loves curling up on your lap or finding a bag to sleep in. The boys adore each other and cannot resist an adventure or cuddling up for a nap together.

Printed in Poland
by Amazon Fulfillment
Poland Sp. z o.o., Wrocław

64978504R00019